KATHLEEN HAGUE

THE LEGEND OF THE
VEERY BIRD

Illustrated by
MICHAEL HAGUE

HARCOURT BRACE JOVANOVICH, PUBLISHERS

SAN DIEGO   NEW YORK   LONDON

For Grandmother Waggoner
—Kathleen and Michael

Requests for permission to make copies of any part
of the work should be mailed to: Permissions,
Harcourt Brace Jovanovich, Publishers, Orlando,
Florida 32887

Library of Congress Cataloging in Publication Data
Hague, Kathleen.
    The legend of the Veery bird.
    Summary: The beautiful Keeper of the Forest
helps a gentle, reclusive youth when he most needs
it and gives the world a bird with a beautiful voice.
        1. Children's stories, American.
        [1. Birds—Fiction]
I. Hague, Michael, ill. II. Title.
PZ7.H1246Le 1985   [E]   84-19732
ISBN 0-15-243824-6

Printed in the United States of America

First edition   A B C D E

The paintings in this book were done in
    watercolors and gouache on illustration board.
The text type was set on the Compugraphic 8204
    in Garamond Light by Hillcrest Graphics,
    San Diego, California.
The display type was set by phototypositor by
    Thompson Type, San Diego, California.
Color separations were made by Heinz Weber, Inc.,
    Los Angeles, California.
Printed by Holyoke Lithograph, Springfield,
    Massachusetts.
Bound by A. Horowitz & Sons, Fairfield,
    New Jersey.
Production supervision by Warren Wallerstein.

THE LEGEND OF THE
VEERY BIRD

STORYTELLER'S NOTE

The sweetest bird songs are found in the deepest forests. They belong to the tiny veery, a thrush of tawny brown. Using classic elements of tragedy, romance, transformation, and magic, this original fairy talc has been fashioned in honor of the veery bird.

—K.H.

Some time ago, in a small village near the edge of a large forest, there lived a man and his wife. They had a handsome young son named Veery. Veery was a timid and quiet child. His parents thought that he would outgrow his shyness, but as he grew older, he became even more self-conscious. When he spoke, he stuttered. Many of the village children taunted him and delighted in seeing him blush when spoken to.

It was not long before he refused to go far from home, and he shunned anyone who tried to speak with him. His parents worried about their son, but because they loved him dearly they tried to understand and left him to himself as he wished.

Veery spent hours alone in the nearby forest. He loved the dense shade it provided. He would stretch out upon the damp ground and close his eyes and smell the lush green that surrounded him and listen to the forest's sounds. At night he watched as the stars danced with one another in the dark skies. He smiled when they peered down at him.

Veery felt comfortable and safe within the forest's boundaries. He spent more and more of his time there, observing the passage of the seasons one by one and sharing with the forest the changes thus brought.

9

One day while Veery was in the forest, his father had an accident and died. When Veery returned home, he found his mother crying. She told him of the terrible tragedy. He could scarcely believe that his father was gone. He tried to comfort his mother, but he could not find what he thought were fitting words. He felt helpless.

Veery grieved that he had not told his father of his love for him. He was ashamed that he could not speak of it now to his mother.

Veery was frightened and felt more alone now than he had ever felt before. He rushed from the house, seeking again the familiar refuge of the forest.

Veery was so consumed with his sorrow that he did not hear the figure approach. It was a young woman, the Keeper of the Forest. She was graceful and beautiful and had the gentle smile of one bewitched. She had secretly watched this handsome and gentle young man during his frequent visits to her forest. She had been taken by the sight of him and had lost her heart to him long ago. And now, seeing him in such a sorrowful state, she could no longer stand to remain in hiding.

"Gentle, handsome young man," she said, "please tell me what troubles you. I cannot stand to see you so distraught."

Veery quickly looked up, startled at the sound of a human voice in the forest. He was astounded by her great beauty. For a brief moment, he forgot his grief. Still, he could not speak. Soon he lapsed into sobs again.

She sighed. One as charming as he should be singing as the birds do. His heart should be light and soar as if it had wings. She spoke again. "You have over these years become a part of my forest and thus a part of me. Now tell me your troubles. I am bound as care-taker of everything here to make it right."

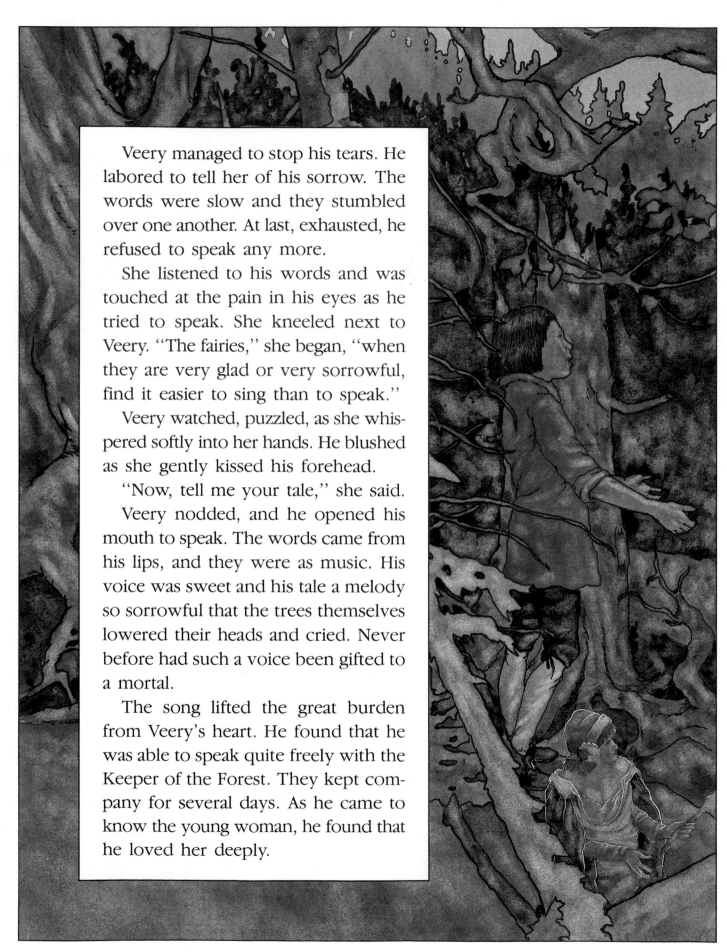

Veery managed to stop his tears. He labored to tell her of his sorrow. The words were slow and they stumbled over one another. At last, exhausted, he refused to speak any more.

She listened to his words and was touched at the pain in his eyes as he tried to speak. She kneeled next to Veery. "The fairies," she began, "when they are very glad or very sorrowful, find it easier to sing than to speak."

Veery watched, puzzled, as she whispered softly into her hands. He blushed as she gently kissed his forehead.

"Now, tell me your tale," she said.

Veery nodded, and he opened his mouth to speak. The words came from his lips, and they were as music. His voice was sweet and his tale a melody so sorrowful that the trees themselves lowered their heads and cried. Never before had such a voice been gifted to a mortal.

The song lifted the great burden from Veery's heart. He found that he was able to speak quite freely with the Keeper of the Forest. They kept company for several days. As he came to know the young woman, he found that he loved her deeply.

Then the time came when Veery knew he should return home to see his mother. He tried to persuade his lady to come with him, but she said she could not. Veery was afraid to leave, because he might not see her again.

But, she promised that he need only to return to the forest and wish for her company, and she would appear. She told him that she would be there as long as he promised to sing only for her. Veery promised and left for his mother's house.

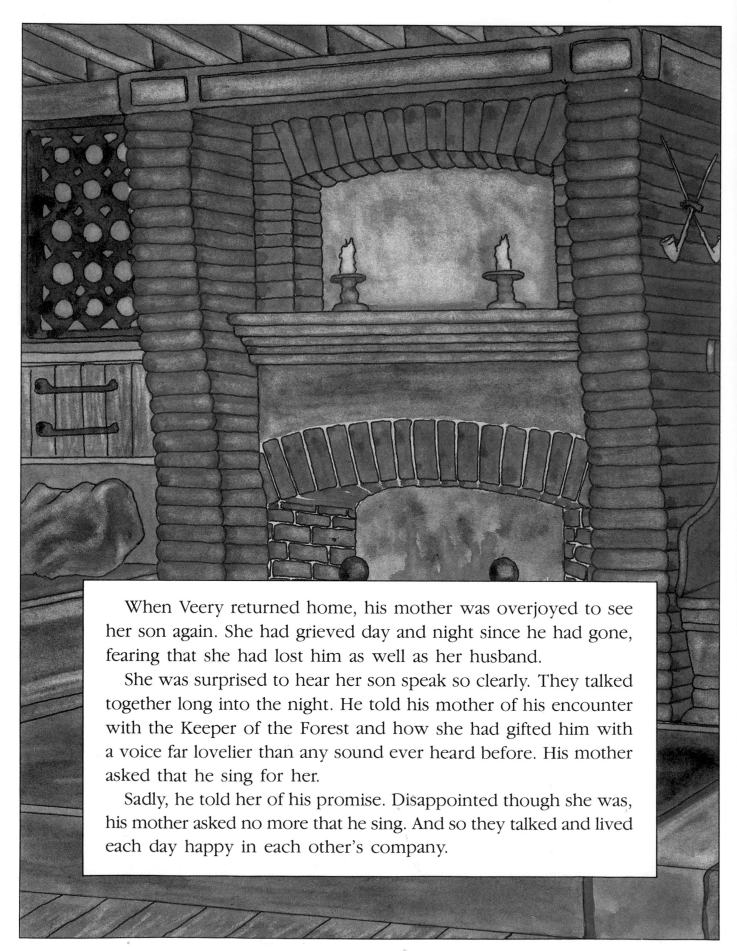

When Veery returned home, his mother was overjoyed to see her son again. She had grieved day and night since he had gone, fearing that she had lost him as well as her husband.

She was surprised to hear her son speak so clearly. They talked together long into the night. He told his mother of his encounter with the Keeper of the Forest and how she had gifted him with a voice far lovelier than any sound ever heard before. His mother asked that he sing for her.

Sadly, he told her of his promise. Disappointed though she was, his mother asked no more that he sing. And so they talked and lived each day happy in each other's company.

Veery frequently visited the forest. As
he had been told, he needed only to
wish for the Keeper of the Forest and
she would appear. Years passed, and as
he had promised, Veery only sang for
his lady.

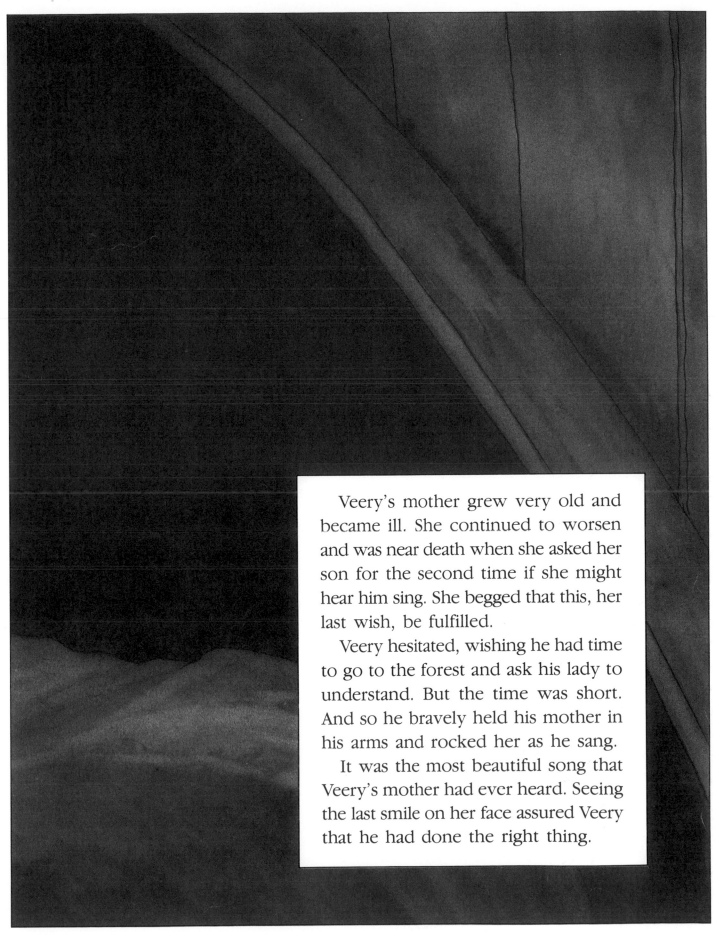

Veery's mother grew very old and became ill. She continued to worsen and was near death when she asked her son for the second time if she might hear him sing. She begged that this, her last wish, be fulfilled.

Veery hesitated, wishing he had time to go to the forest and ask his lady to understand. But the time was short. And so he bravely held his mother in his arms and rocked her as he sang.

It was the most beautiful song that Veery's mother had ever heard. Seeing the last smile on her face assured Veery that he had done the right thing.

Veery was grieved by his mother's death. He left his house for the forest to explain why he had broken his promise. He reached the trees and wished for his lady to appear. But she did not.

Veery searched everywhere, without success. The Keeper of the Forest had vanished. All the sorrow of his life tumbled down around him. He dropped to the ground, wishing death would take him, too. He searched the sky for an answer, hoping only for the chance to see his love once more.

It was night when Veery awoke. The hurt in his heart had become something more tangible. His legs ached and his arms felt heavy and awkward. He could not manage to raise himself up off the ground.

It was very dark, and he could not make out what was covering him as he lay. As the moon rose, he was amazed to see tawny feathers covering his body. When he reached to touch their smooth surface, he discovered that the feathers were his own. He had wings!

He closed his eyes and waited to wake from this odd dream. But the passing of hours proved it was not a dream at all. Veery stood, spread wide his newfound wings, and was gathered up into the night sky.

The winds rushed whispering by his face, and the crisp air filled his lungs with rapture. He enjoyed seeing his shadow dance upon the surface of the clouds. He marveled at the patchwork of velvet colors embroidered with streams of silver far below. His wings were strong, and he flew effortlessly. He caught the rising currents, and his heart quickened as he was lifted even higher.

He flew on and on, watching the sun repeat its daily pageantry. He saw smoldering deserts, lakes of glass, massive mountains, and wide expanses of satiny oceans with phosphorescent waves. He did not know what his final destination would be, but he felt instinctively comfortable on his course.

At last his journey ended. He lay down on the ground to rest, and he fell asleep.

The brisk morning breeze was scattering the last of Veery's feathers across the ground when he awoke. He was saddened to find his wings gone. His mind began to go over the past events, trying to figure out what had happened and why. Maybe this had indeed been a dream—or perhaps he had gone mad.

Veery lowered his head into the palms of his hands and let the warm sun fall across his shoulders. He heard someone approach. He looked up, hoping it was someone who could tell him where he was. Veery was stunned to see standing but a few feet away his lady. She smiled and beckoned him to join her. Together they walked, and into a nearby forest they disappeared.

The Keeper of the Forest took Veery away forever. In his place she left a bird she had created and given Veery's same gentle and shy nature and beautiful voice. The bird is called Veery to this day.